W. G. Collingwood

Coniston Tales

W. G. Collingwood

Coniston Tales

ISBN/EAN: 9783337138332

Printed in Europe, USA, Canada, Australia, Japan

Cover: Foto ©Andreas Hilbeck / pixelio.de

More available books at **www.hansebooks.com**

CONISTON TALES.

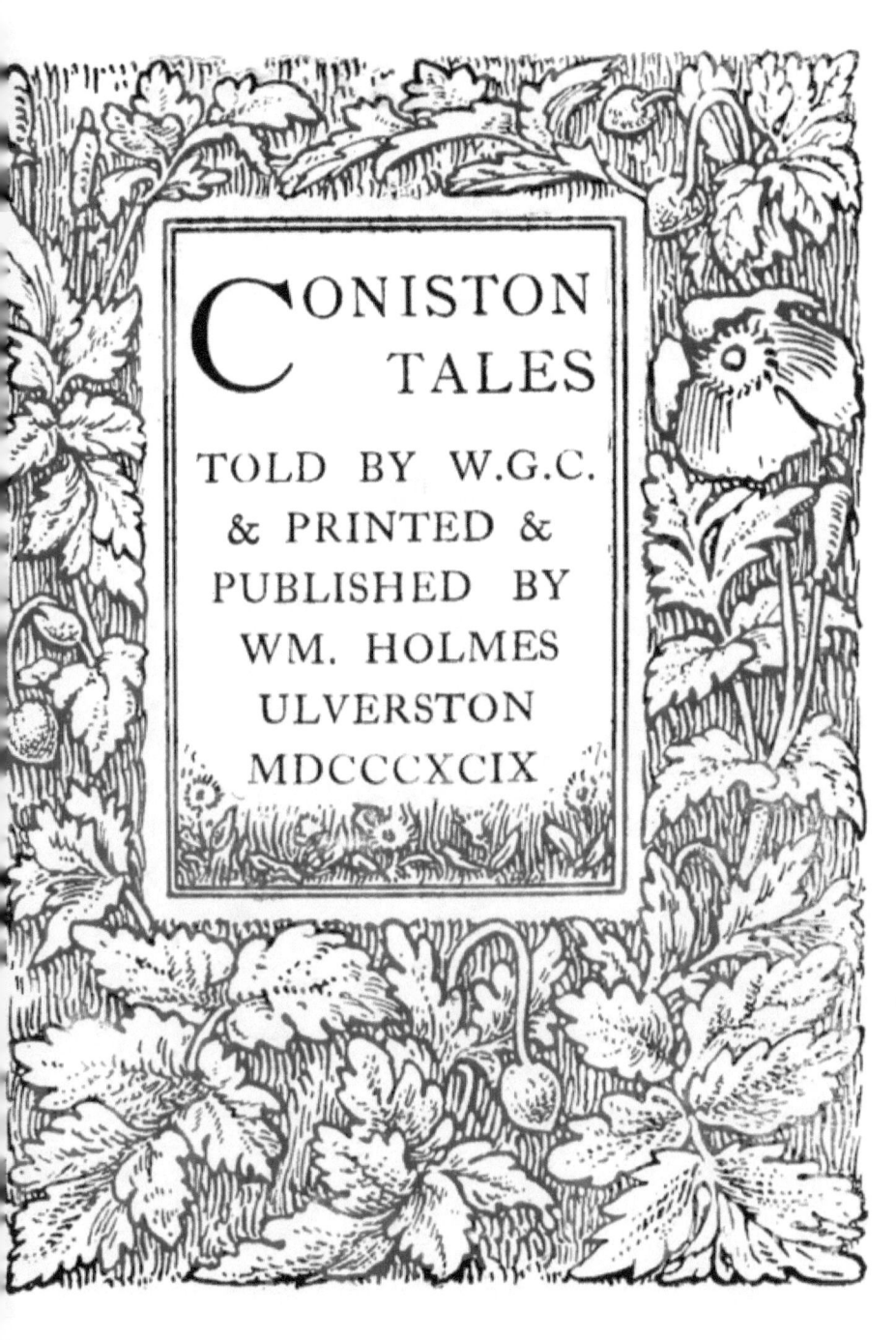

Coniston Tales

TOLD BY W.G.C.
& PRINTED &
PUBLISHED BY
WM. HOLMES
ULVERSTON
MDCCCXCIX

To the Editor of

" *Nothing Much: a Monthly Magazine.*"

It was owing to your encouragement that these sketches were attempted; and it is by your help and permission that they are now reproduced from your pages.   Accept, then, the dedication of our little book from

Your obliged contributor,

W. G. C.

Coniston, April, 1899.

CONTENTS.

THE APOLOGY.

Two poets of old we know,
    Two saga-smiths to-day;
And the one is " Long-ago,"
    And the other is " Far-away."

For the things of Here-and-now,
    And the thoughts of Now-and-here,
They write on the wrinkled brow
    In runes of an evil cheer.

They bid us be up and fight,
    They shout to us " Forth and strive ! "
From the cock-crow, on to the night,
    As long as we stand alive.

But the old-world tale says—" Dream
    Of days that have long gone by,
By the light of the sunrise gleam
    And the glamour of memory."

And over the hills is hope
    And the wonder of distant things,
As the stars in the telescope
    Out-glitter your diamond rings.

So the cares of a weary day
    Fall from us like spring-tide snow,
When we gaze upon Far-away,
    Or dream about Long-ago.

THE CAIRN ON THE MOOR.

It was on Torver moor I lay in the grass; and the sun was hot on my shoulders, and the heat of it scorched my cheek, and my ear tingled where it was touched by the burning. I was lying on an old cairn, stone-built and mortared with moss; the crown of the cairn was dimpled like the crown of a ripe apple, and turf and thyme crept about its foundation. Bees were busy at the thyme; they sailed and stopped, sailed and stopped, and the coming of them was stillness rather than sound. Then a very little breath of wind swept over the moor, and they took their ways, and went. And then, down in the cairn, I heard talking, as it might be on the other side of a door.

*　　　*　　　*　　　*　　　*

"No greater gift is given of man to man. With this the tree that grows thick as thy waist is broken and falls, to hollow for a boat, or to prop thy hut-thatch."

"Give it then to my hand."

"Nay, listen. With this the bone thy teeth have cleaned is made as a thorn, to let out the life of beast or man."

"Give it, I say."

"Nay, hear. With this the oak-stub is hollowed, before one moon grows round, when red-hot stones have been nightly heaped upon it. With this thou tappest softly—so!—the wild wolf's headbone, or maybe a man's, and he is dead."

"It is mine."

" And what mine ? "
" This coat of deerskin."
" That is nothing."
" This necklet of teeth."
" That is little."

" Ho, child, hither ! Leave twining bark-strips and turn thy feet to me. And thou, stranger, look upon her. Fat she is, for she eats fat of deer. Red is her mouth, for she drinks the blood when it is warm. And when the snow is deep, she lies by the fire and none stirs her. The best she has of all, and she is strong as a young wolf."

*　　*　　*　　*　　*

Then I saw the stranger tramping over the moor, and the wind blew ; a tall man, shaggy and fierce; and after him tripped a young girl, lithe and strong, with fair skin, sunburnt, and slim, ungirded waist. Black were her eyes, and gleaming ; and rosy her cheeks, with a tear on each. Her long dark hair streamed away in the wind. On her back she carried the skin sack of the stranger, heavy with its load ; and as he went down to the ford of the gill, he turned to her, and seemed to bid her look well to her burden ; but with no menace ; and she looked at him with soft eyes, as a dog looks.

But by the low turf-thatched hut on the brow of the moor stood the other man, heeding them not at all, but patting and fondling a sharp stone axe, stroking it over as if it had been a living cub of some beast of the hunt. Then he hewed at a log of wood, and the axe stuck in it. He laughed and shouted, and wrested it away.

3

Out of the hut crept a woman, on hands and knees, for the door was low. She stood up and stared around, and shrieked out to the man. He held up his treasure before her eyes, and she sat down and rocked herself and tore her hair.

*   *   *   *   *

There was talking again; it would be in the stranger's hut,—a little, cooing voice :—

"Go then, and come back with the greatest buck on the mountains. The fire shall burn, and I will make thee taste savoury meat."

"It is thee I would eat, bird: soft to my hands, and to my mouth sweet as honey."

"And to-morrow?"

"To-morrow I would lie still and taste what I had eaten."

"And the third day?"

"The third day I would set fire to rafter and thatch, and go in the smoke, thy bones and mine together, thy flesh and mine, to the stars."

"Nay now, fool; leave this, and away to the hunting."

"Come thou with me. We will hunt together, and I will show thee a nest of eaglets."

"What? And who will get firewood, and fetch water, and pick red heather for thy filthy black hut?"

"We two, afterwards?"

"By moonlight? Go, rough bear, go; and be as men are. Am I not a woman, and thy wife?"

*   *   *   *   *

Then it was moonlight. The mist lay flat along the valley, as if the waters had risen to the brink of the moor. Outside the hut a fire burnt, and she threw sticks upon it, and stones: and now and then raked out a stone red-hot, to cast it into a great earthen pot where water was bubbling. She looked over the moor. Other huts, hard by, lay silent; and their fires smouldered and smoked up to the sky. She looked up at the crags. They were black, and nothing stirred betwixt them and her. The moon waded through the clouds, and a red star shone in the fringe of the moon-burr.

There was one coming over the moor in the mist. She clapped her hands, and ran to meet him, crying out shrilly like a curlew. She ran and stopped. He was gone. Her knees shook as she came trembling back to the hut, and to the sinking fire.

The moon was over the crags. She climbed upon a hillock and looked out again. There was one standing on the hillock over against her. She plunged through the heather and panted up the brow: but he was gone. Her teeth chattered as she came back to the hut; and the fire was failing.

The moon was set now: only the red star stood upon the edge of the crags. She climbed again to watch the brown moor, and lo! one stooped at the very door of the hut, stooping as if to enter. He was plain to see, between her and the firelight. She flew down the slope, and fell into the doorway; but no one was there; and she lay by the dying fire, hardly able to throw twig

5

after twig upon it. But this she must do, till he came.
Then the dawn arose; and then the morning.

* * * * *

"What, woman? Is thy man away?"
"Oh, neighbour, where is he?"
"Who should know but thou?"
"I drove him out to hunt."
"A hunting he will be."
"But I saw him cross the moor."
"It was a deer."
"But I saw him stand on yon brow."
"It was no more than a stone."
"But I saw him come in at this door."
"Nay then, get thee gone to the wise man."

* * * * *

Then an old man came, brown-skinned and tanned
all over, as if he had lain for a hundred years in a peat-
bog. His tawny white hair hung to his waist; his
beard clothed him below it, and the hair of his limbs
was white on the brown. He had a hollow cobble in
his hand, and over it for a lid was a lucky-stone, such a
bit of slate with an unmade hole in it as you find on the
topmost top of Coniston fells. He took red embers in
his finger-tips, and set them in the hollow of the stone;
and white smoke curled up through the hole in the lid.
He crept into her hut, and the door was shut upon him.
She sat weeping outside, and her hair lay in her lap.
Within the hut there was a stirring, and harsh singing,
and cries. They bade her ask, now or never, of the

6

wise man made strong in his wisdom.

*   *   *   *   *

" Father, where is he?"

" Search."

" Where shall I turn?"

" Higher."

" Dost thou see him?"

" I see him."

" Oh, tell me."

" Betwixt crag and water."

" Does he stir?"

" He sleeps."

" O give me tokens."

" Black and white the stream falls, red and white he lies."

*   *   *   *   *

She was clambering over the giant screes, calling and crying. Aloft, the cloven crags hung huge above her. Beneath was a black, still tarn. Over against her rose the mountain into the cloud. The screes moved under her feet, that bled from sharp stones, and her knees were red from rough rasping. There was no answer to her cry but what the rocks gave back, shouting to her, all around. Every cranny of the great rock-slide she searched, and rubbed her eyes with torn hand, and clambered forward. Then into a clift she fell, and in her fall she clasped him.

*   *   *   *   *

" Oh, man of mine, strong man of mine, hunter of the

7

wolf, and the red deer, and the roe!

"How have I lost thee, how have I followed thee, how have I found thee again?

"Oh, light of my eyes; oh, drink of my mouth; oh, fire of the heart in my body!

"Where is the glance of thee? where is the breath of thee? where is the warmth of thy cold, cold breast?

"A great thing he gave; a little thing he got; but he took me to his dwelling, and I am his.

"How shall I call thee? how shall I awaken thee? the life-blood has run through the crannies of the rocks.

"The grey rocks have eaten thee, the sharp rocks have torn thee; as a bear, as a wolf, growling over a kid of the goats.

"This I know; this will I do. Be strong, my shoulders, as an oak; be hard, my broken feet, as the stones of the crags.

"I will carry him back to the kinsfolk: I will build him the red sleeping-place of the silent: I will lie down beside him, and hold him fast; and we shall go up together!"

*   *   *   *   *

Round about the fire of the dead they stood, the wild folk of the fell: and the heather blazed up with a smothering smoke. There was a great cry, shrill as a curlew's; and a low cry, soft as a dove's; and they looked on one another and nodded with their heads.

When the fire had died away, out of the embers they plucked a few bones, and a handful of white ashes, and all that was left of a true heart.

On the spot of the burning they left them, in a rude urn of clay. Men laid stones around, and roofed the spot over with unhewn stones. Women tore their hair and beat their bosoms, keening and clamouring around the cairn on the moor.

*   *   *   *   *

The bees sailed by to the thyme, and stopped, and clung about the grasses. The sun stood over Dow Crags, and the moon was rising, soft, behind the long fir-woods of Monk Coniston, dreamy and warm in the evening light. It was an easy pillow for a sleeping head, that moss-grown, dimpled pile, and turf-invaded base of the still unviolated tomb.

"Ah!" said I, rising, "three thousand years ago— or in dreamland—such hearts may be found!"

But I was young, then, and had many things to learn.

THE GREAT CIRCLE.

He was father and chief of the Tykes,
    when the Tykes were a clan;
They chaunted him Son of the Hound
    their mightiest man:
In the days when the corries were ice
    and the summits were snow,
And the valleys were smothered in birch
    and the levels in flow.
He was master of borran and lyth,
    he was lord of the moor,
And he followed the hunt like a dog
    for his scent was as sure;
With breath as unbroken, and muscle
    as ropy and full,
And the beard and the brow of an ape,
    and the voice of a bull

When the boar of the swamp was at bay
    it was he that ran in;
When the Cave-dweller bellowed and boxed,
    it was he took the skin;
And when strangers came up through the woods
    from the far-lying plain,
It was he that heaved rocks at their heads
    till they vanished again.
His desire was a law to his tribe,
    his saying was good:

He took what he fancied of weapons,
   or women, or food;
He gave what he wearied of, smote
   what he angered with,—slew
Foe that fled, friend that fell, child that cried:
   and to plead, was *taboo*.

So the creature grew heavy and fat,
   and at last, unaware,
He was caught, he was speared, he was slain,
   like his brother the bear.
And with wailing, and faces flint-scored,
   and anointed with mud,
His kinspeople buried him—*here*,
   where the peat drank his blood.
They gave him a spear, that the spirit
   might hunt for his meat,
And a slave newly-slain at his head,
   and a wife at his feet:
And leaving him housed in the cairn,
   their last offering they made,
Of drink in a bowl, and of flesh
   for the peace of the shade.

Now wonders began.   For the folk
   climbed hillward at morn,
To wit was the offering accepted
   or wasted in scorn:
And lo! the bowl empty, the platter
   lay cleared on the ground,

And two long grey wolves of the wood
    stretched out by the mound.
"He was stirring," they whispered, "at night:
    he has drunken, and fed;
He has smitten a stroke at the beasts,
    and is back to his bed!"
And they prided themselves on their chief,
    filled platter and bowl,
And abode between worship and awe
    for the terrible soul.

So the days wore to winter; the dark
    out-wearied the moon,
And the sun-setting nightly drew nearer
    the mark of the noon:
And she that should go with the grave-meal,
    a withered old wife,
Nay, she would not: let younger folk fare:
    she was feared of her life.
She had seen—What? a wolf? Well, a bear?—
    she had heard—What? the dead?
She knew not: her heart was as water:
    her knees failed: she fled.
So a dare-devil lass cried "Who fears?"
    and forth she would go:
And they found her next day by the grave,
    with her face in the snow.

Then they trembled, and whispered, and pointed,
    and fled in affright;

And they hid in their hovels, and listened,
  and quaked through the night.
But when celandine glittered, and daisies
  peeped out on the grave,
The dread of the dark passed away,
  for the spring made them brave.
Till at last on an eve came one
  through twilitten ways,
With foam on his beard, and his eyes
  yet afire with amaze:
"I have seen him!—he chased me!—he caught me!
  I fought him!" he cried:
"I wrestled,—I threw him!" he panted,
  and, speaking, he died.

Then the elders sat grimly in conclave,
  their feet to the fire,
With the Druid, their medicine-man,
  in his magic attire,—
Strange feathers and furs of creatures
  they dreaded the most,
And a snake-skin for belt, and a mask
  would frighten a ghost.
He was wizard, and prophet, and priest,
  and he knew what was wise
When war was afoot between men
  and the folk of the skies.
So he lay on the turf, and was silent,
  and rising at last,

Spoke out, of the salve that should heal
    the wounds of the past.

"There are stones on the fell, there are slabs
    as huge as a steer:
Go find them and fetch them.   Ye cannot?—
    no matter: ye hear!
How lead you the bear that is slain?—
    ye call yourselves men,
And heave with a song at the cords
    by ten and by ten.
There are thatch-ropes of hide to your roofs,
    go bind them around:
There are rafters, go lay them beneath
    that they roll on the ground:
So build you a rampart of rock
    in a ring to the tomb,
That he bide in his house, and leave troubling:
    lo! this for his doom."

He was architect also, the Druid:
    he scored out the line,
And planned what none else of his age
    had the wit to divine:
And they chaunted the song of his art
    as they toiled in the blaze,—
The art of the Builder in Stone,
    the first of his days.
And the soul of the terrible dead
    in his grave was at rest:

And the nights of his people were peaceful,
    their mornings were blest;
And less than a little they dreamed
    of the alien eyes
That should stare at their work with amaze,
    in this world of the wise.

OF THE MINES IN THE MOUNTAINS:

A Greek Letter

WRITTEN ABOUT 85 A.D.

[NOTE. Demetrius was a real person, and so was his supposed correspondent. The tablet he dedicated to Oceanus and Tethys I have seen in the Museum at York. Mention of his studies in Britain is made by Plutarch. We do not know that the Coniston mines were actually worked by the Romans, though many writers have affirmed as much. Perhaps the iron-mines in Low Furness were known to them, and worked even still earlier; for at Stainton, two polished stone celts were found in "the old men's workings." In many other parts of England, the Romans certainly mined and smelted, and their coins and pottery have been discovered in the heaps of slag and rubbish where they worked.]

Demetrius, the scribe, to Ammonius, master of philosophy; health and happiness. Many a time it has come into my mind, O Ammonius, to send thee word of my latest wanderings in this isle of Britain: but the distance, and the wildness of this barbarous country, and the irregularity of messengers have prevailed. But now it seems I can pay the debt: for know that I am come to the shore of the uttermost parts, to a haven whence to-morrow a ship will sail, venturing forth like Perseus winging his way from the unknown mountains of Atlas, committing itself like the bark of Ulysses to the streams of encircling ocean, in the amazing hope of revisiting Iberia and the pillars of Heracles, and so through the happier waters of our own sea, making for Rome.

Thence to Delphi is as it were but a step; so that even this frail waxed tablet may come to thy honoured hands. The master mariner to whom I spoke but now, laughed at my wonderment when I asked him what chance he had of reaching port. Said he, "With fair wind and good fortune, in two months or so we shall be eating grapes on the quay at Ostia: never a doubt, saving reverence due to the Nereids: and I," said he with a grin, "am no Hylas." But indeed a wonderful place is this little harbour*: five years ago a desert of spreading sandhills by the grey and many-sounding sea; or at least a village of the wildest barbarians, who in frail barks of 'basket'—so they call it—covered with bulls' hides, essay the fishery of herring and of cod,—yea, even attack the porpoise and the seal. Then comes our great Agricola marching through estuary and forest, opening out dense ways and lightless tracks for the rays of wisdom and the arts of life to enter in. With eagle eye he sees that the haven was fair, being a landlocked pool where three rivers meet, and a narrow opening to the hyperboreal expanse of storm. Note by the way that hereabouts they find pearls, though such as I have seen to-night be but little and internally brownish of hue, with no more than a dull gleam upon them. But with a word our Julius bids a camp arise; and lo! a town, well placed, defensible, and for such a climate neither unfit nor uninhabitable. Yonder, they say,—I saw it not,—one beholds the isle of Mona: and from this port go three roads,—

*Ravenglass.

17

to the south, to the north, and to the west,—whereby the goods of the merchant and the sinews of war are carried on the backs of men and horses far into the heart of the land. Here then at the consummation of my travel through woods and wilds I am greeted by the delights of life: supper not wholly uneatable, being a sheldrake, thought a delicacy by these natives, and with it a salmon and oysters. There is a roof above me fairly built: a couch to lie upon, and—wonder of wonders!—a bath within a few paces of the door. What is no less welcome, I find converse of human beings unlike the apes of the mountains. Think not I mean the same breed with those of Africa, but creatures that are not far removed. Thou sayest, even apes are not too mean nor too unclean for thy disciple to regard with the eye of inquiry: be it so; and indeed I have sought to take the measure of these Gadelic monsters, even to the gauging of their poor wits, and the probing of their shallow ideas of things they ignorantly assert concerning the gods. But the mere sound of a Greek or even a Roman voice cheers me, after the painful solecisms of barbarous guides, and the interpreted stammerings of the more uncouth mountaineers. "Ah me!" have I often said, as I strove to hear their various and incomprehensible babbling, "who shall interpret the interpreters!" I call them apes, but in jest. Thou knowest I scorn them not wholly in my heart; for as the Roman says, "Homo sum," and so forth. Now wilt thou ask, where have I been? in what wilds? among what savages? finding what adventures? My Ammonius, among the Gadeli, for so my apes are called; and in their savagest hills. Mountains I know, and thou knowest: for do not the mountains rise behind Tarsus, my native town, city of great men? and do they not encircle thy sacred home of Delphi? But what is the great Parnassus' self to these they call Skudau, and Elbelin, and the Pens and Kathars and such-like names innumerable in their jargon? Thinkest thou I compare them for their size? not so: for in mere altitude I reckon Taurus or the Heliconian summit at twice their import-ance. Thinkest thou for their prospects? I smile. Never was sight more horrible. For sheer lack of aught that may make travelling endurable; for cold and wet, for hunger and toil, for roughness of rock and pathless-ness of waste, for treacherous swamp and tangled forest, and above all for danger of yet unsubdued savages, fiercer than their wolves and wild bulls,—for these no Caucasus nor Alps may be compared with that I have gone through to-day; and I shake the dust,—nay, the mud of them, from my weary feet. For being sent, as thou knowest, O Ammonius, by Augustus Domitian, whom the gods preserve, to search out the resources of this island, and to add unknown wealth to the glory of the empire, I came to Eburacum. How I travelled; what honourable reception I had from the governor; how I laboured to approve myself worthy of his welcome, teaching for a season in the schools which he,—greatly (in my judgment) hoping—has founded for the better sort of barbarians;—all this have I written and sent by the imperial messenger. To the daring seaman who pushes forth into the unknown to-morrow I entrust these less valued lines. Know then that Agricola the governor, having travelled in these parts, and having sought information from the natives, bade me search diligently for certain iron and copper of which tales were told. I heard and obeyed. By the road his centurions had made I travelled through the land of the Brigantes, making all haste across the less rugged but not more fertile hill-country, until I came to a great bay, called by the Britons Mor Kam, which is to say 'the crooked sea.' Thence over wide wet sands. Thou knowest, in these places the sea falls twice a day, and twice comes roaring back to take up its place. Was it that which Homer meant in saying 'the Streams of Ocean,' and not only the currents and whirlpools thereof? I leave this by the way to thy better judgment. Now across the sands there is a well-known road, by the coasts of the Sistuntii: and where the successive estuaries of Lona and Kanta and Lebena give place to dry land, the road is made over white rocks that put me in mind of the white crags of Greece. Forgive the comparison! for to an exile even the likeness of stone with stone takes the eye. And these white rocks, whereof I bring with me morsels, are assuredly like our marble, though coarser in grain, being well fitted for burning to lime. There is also good abundance of a tophaceous marl, fit for agriculture. Now when I had passed the sands without mishap, trusting to my guides, I came to a road well made in the red earth, through an undulating land; and on a brow above a little valley found lodging in the station founded by our Agricola*. Thereabouts the rocks are red; and it needed no witness to show me iron lying somewhere hidden in the limestone. Not to weary thee with many a day's toil, I found good ore, and marked the spots. Showing my tablets of authority to the prefect, I bade him set men to work digging it in places better and more profitable than those where the ignorant natives had scratched the soil with rude stone tools, smelting the red ore in ruder hearths. Thence, after repose, seven days ago—it seems a month of nights—I set forth, hearing that copper was found in the mountains. My heart failed me to venture into those trackless wilds; but duty, and the service I owe, impelled me to risk my life: for am I not as it were the soldier of philosophy? Therefore I set forth with a good company, and well armed, given me by the prefect, under a centurion responsible for my safe conduct, to whom was added a ragged crew of aborigines who partly for fear and slavish awe, and partly tempted by promises—for Agricola's comity has taught me to deal friendly even with these apes—had taken oath on all they held sacred,—of which more hereafter,—to show me where copper might be. For thou mayest believe to seek mines in these mountains, be a man ever so expert, is seeking knots in a rush, without he have some forewarning of their place. In a little while we left the plain, if plain it be called, being

*He seems to mean Dalton-in-Furness.

21

but the shelf of shore along another estuary. Forgive the comparison again!—but I held it not unlike the coasts of thy home, in that mountains stand over against mountains, with inlets of the sea between. Then we struck into the wilderness, and forced our way through woods of oak and beech; the olive is unknown in this region, nor does the cypress grow, though the juniper is as it were a mockery of it; and we passed over tracts of heather, which (wonderful to relate) blooms even here. It gladdened me to breathe its well-remembered fragrance. Much club-moss is found on the hills, and plucked by our Britons for charms, according to their religion. Before us were ever the distant mountains, purple on the afternoon sky. The multitude of birds astonished me. Of lesser kinds were flights innumerable: but what thou wouldst admire is the wild peacock of the north, a great bird of many colours that makes its nest in these moors.* At evening, so wearied was I, for I could not always ride on my horse, the ways being far too rough, and I often rode on the back of an unsavoury Gadelus—pity me, Ammonius!—so wearied was I that I fell supine upon the heather which they gathered for my couch, and so continued until the sun was high. That day I came to a lake, long and narrow, embosomed in the wooded hills. Here the fresh-water fishery might be to some profit, if ever men were brought to live so far away from the world: but who can dwell in such a place, even to eat fresh trout? Upon heathery wastes I did indeed see

*The Capercailzie.

huts of the Gadeli, and smoke arising. I bade my men catch one of these same apes, that I might see whether he had the form of humanity: and one they caught asleep in his lair. He blinked at me from under a shaggy red thatch of matted hair; and truly, though thou mayest exclaim and doubt, he might have passed, were he washed and combed, for one of those red Galatians, long limbed and barbarous of aspect, whom I have seen come down to Tarsus. But he would answer no word to all questions, and my men, being used to such cattle, began to twist his arms and chastise him, that he should speak. But I, more humane, as becomes thy disciple and a follower of our Julius, bade them somewhat sharply to desist. On which released he was gone in the twinkling of an eye: skipping among the tall bushes of heather, and hardly discernible at the distance of a stone's throw. One of my men, recovering himself, did indeed sling a bullet after him, but it seemed to fail of the mark: for which the centurion smote him down, and promised discipline to those that had let the ape go free. Thou mightest say, my master, that they were not wholly to blame. I will bear it in mind, if indeed punishment be not already meted out. And yet in these wilds there is little time for ethical disputations and the nice balancing of motives, as we use in the schools. The soul of a man deserts his head, and seems to travel to the finger-joints of his right hand; which, being prompt, has a justice of its own in this land of Britain. So thus I came into the very heart of the mountains, beside a roaring stream that led into a dell exceeding narrow. I passed therein with fear and trembling; for the rocks were high above my head, and great stones lay around, but lately fallen and shattered. By the mercy of the gods we came through, but only to find rocks still more frightful and dangerous, reaching to the sky all around, and great waterfalls hanging from them, and clouds covering their tops,— who knows how lofty and threatening? I put up a prayer to the deities of the place and to the genius of Augustus, as well I might; and took heart somewhat: for true it is, in spite of doubting, that holy beings dwell in these sacred recesses. Have I not felt their awe? Even my soldiers,—nay, even the apes themselves, believe it,—held breath, and seemed to fear. Now the rock of these mountains is black: and in places I found (for we spent the night even there) certain pillars of stone hexagonal, such as are seen only in land near a burning mountain, for such is my experience. Seeing which, I enquired if fire had ever been known to burst from the earth. They assured me that no such thing was in any old stories or songs of the people. And yet there are great craters in these hills,* like that of Vesuvius; some-times filled with water, which might seem to have quenched the native fire. And yet, thou knowest how Vesuvius, so long quiet, burst forth but five years ago, and with what terrible consequences. I braved every danger, and confident in my mission and the protection

*It was clever of him to notice this, but he was quite mistaken, as every schoolboy knows nowadays.

24

of the gods, explored the uttermost cranny of this tartarean gulf. It is in these crannies that copper is found. A white streak of hard stone, sparkling like alabaster, and a glimmer as of gold in it,—or a streak of soft red earth in the solid rock, stained with green spots,—betrays the metal. Some little holes had been dug here and there by the natives, but as before the best places were untouched. These I noted, and the manner of finding them again; and shortly (fortune favouring) shall send men to open out mines, and with due authority to work them for copper. But the lamp burns low. My sailor snores at the door, waiting this hour for the letter I scribble hastily. The tablets will hold no more than must suffice to tell thee how, after a day's journey through hills even as frightful, I came to a fort on a steep, lofty tongue of land in the midst of the mountains, where the builders are still at work.* There I was well received, and resting for one night, travelled more easily by a road even now in making, through a valley unspeakably hideous and wild, beside a river, whereof when I asked the name they could tell nothing but Usg or Esk, which is no more than to say 'water.' Such is the state of these barbarians. And now after short repose I must again venture forth into these mountains, for I hear talk of still richer mines in them. May Oceanus and Tethys, whom I here behold face to face under the stars, send me safe into civilized regions! May all good gods be with thee! Farewell.

*Hardknott Castle, of course!

Salute the young Plutarch for me, and tell him that I, who laughed once, follow him now, in carrying tablets with me, and noting all new things in the moment of seeing them.

THE THREE GODMOTHERS.

In days of yore on a morn in Yule
   There were folk at a christening :
The priest was robed, and the stoup was filled,
   For the child of the Angle king.

The child was born at the mirk midnight,
   And lapped in the snow-white lawn,
And holden forth from bower to kirk
   Before the break of dawn.

'Now who stand out to speak the word,
   And stead him at the font?
And who shall be his godmother
   As Christian folk are wont?'

And lo ! beside the holy step
   Three ladies standing fair ;
Raven-locks and Chestnut-curls
   And she with the golden hair.

Raven-hair with the purple robe,
   And Chestnut-curls with the plaid,
And Goldilocks with the great white limbs,
   And the bearskin, and the blade.

'Now take the child, and make the pledge,
   And vow the gossip-vow.'
They lifted a hand to the stars above
   And laid it on his brow.

27

And Raven-hair she gave him a gift,
    That was a kingly wand;
And Chestnut-curls she gave him a gift,
    The harp was in her hand:

And Goldilocks she gave him a gift,
    And a smile was on her lip,
When his little red hand shut hard and fast
    On the tiller of a ship.

'Now who be these that none saw come,
    And none have seen depart?
Were these thy saints, O priest, from heaven,
    Or wights of wizard art?'

'Nay, neither saints, O king, from heaven,
    Nor wights of wicked birth;
But the greatest of all the powers that be,
    And dwell in middle earth.

'For one was queen of the South country,
    And one of the Western realm,
And one was queen of the Northern coasts
    That bare the long-ship's helm.

'And she that gave a golden rod,
    She has given the ruler's dower,
To hold the world in weal and peace
    With the heritage of power.

28

'And she that gave the chorded harp,
    She has given a secret spell
To call the tears to an angel's eyes
    And a smile to souls in hell.

'And she that gave the tiller-haft,
    She has given a heart of oak,
To drive the horses of the storm
    In the sturdy sea-king's yoke!'

The king laughed out for very pride,
    And snapped his thumb in glee;
But the priest looked forth to the rising sun,
    And he signed with his fingers three.

'Hail to thee, child of the Angle-folk,
    And the gifts that the world has given!
Wield them, and prosper—till thou forget
The gift I have brought thee is greater yet—
    The cross of thy Lord in Heaven.'

A MIRACLE OF ST. CUTHBERT

(ABOUT 680 A.D.)

[There is neither history nor legend of St. Cuthbert at Coniston. The whole story is a might-have-been. But there is nothing in it that might *not* have been; and Reginald of Durham might have written it somewhat as follows.]

HIC INCIPIT MIRACULUM QUOD BEATUS CUTHBERTUS IN COUPLANDIA EST OPERATUS.

Of that holy man Cuthbert, pleasant and profitable it is to read: and though the pen refuses to set down all the journeyings he made, and the words he spoke, and the wonderful actions he performed, and many are perforce omitted from the tale of the reckoning, yet it is not ungrateful to add one other to the chapters of his life, as it has been recounted to us by scribes of old time.

For whereas Cuthbert was made bishop over the land of the Cumbrians, after that King Ecgfrith had subdued them to his arms, it so happened that the pious monarch, impelled by divine desires, gave into the hand of the holy man all that country which is called Cartmel, with such Britons as dwelt therein, to hold in his free possession for aliment and for comfort in his many journeyings, when the office and work of his ministry called him hither and thither.

Now being at the city of Carlisle, it was borne in upon him to visit this new possession and to set it in order spiritually no less than temporally: and on the way to confirm the churches, exhorting the faithful, rousing the

30

sluggards, and compelling all to the faithful following of their high calling. Therefore setting forth with those who never were absent from him, night or day, he passed through the wood of the English until he came to the mountains: where on an island in a remote lake dwelt his dear friend Herbert in hermitage.

Having visited him and held communion with him, the holy man took his way fearless through the valleys of the rugged hills and untenanted rocks, by a path nigh obliterated of ancient times, going ever southward through the forest of Coupland: for by this road his guides, the shepherds of the mountains, assured him he might the soonest come into Cartmel. And traversing a great valley, and thereafter hills of no small terror and difficulty, he came at last to a hidden place among lofty rocks, where, beside a lake of water, copper is digged in the bowels of the earth. And because this working of metals belongs by right to the king and is done at his command under officers appointed by him, the place is named Cuninges-tune, i.e. the town or village of the king.

In this place, among rude people of the mines, and certain Welsh who tended a few sheep and goats upon the greener pastures of the desert hills, there was a church in those days, of no great size or beauty: being but the inartificial building of the priest who tenanted it. For he was an Irishman, and one of that sect and heresy with which even the blessed Cuthbert himself being infect in his extreme youth and ignorance, did afterwards forsake, and under the guidance of holy church, combat and overcome, and utterly extirpate from all the territory of the English. It was but some five and twenty years before, that Bega the abbess had built the house of nuns on the promontory that by the British is called Baruth, that is, the Red Headland, being come over from Ireland with her following to spread the gospel in these deserts. Nor is she that Bega of Hackness of whom Bede makes mention, as some do vainly imagine; but another, who from her house of Saint Bee's, as the folk of the place call it, sent forth one and another into the mountains to shepherd the flock of the Lord, and to lead wild goats of the hills as lambs to the fold. Yet even so, her followers were uninstructed in the truth as it is taught to us; baptizing with but one immersion, and shaving the hair across the forehead as the Irish used, and keeping the Paschal feast with vitiated calendar at uncanonical time and season; though earnest withal in their manner, and learned in the Scriptures and in holy arts.

This poor man, then, being come through the wilds to the aforesaid place, built there his cell of wattle and daubing, as some maintain; though others will have it of stones plucked from the rough ground and rudely piled together into the form of a round hut,—no fitting temple, but such as he had ability to raise,—at the ford where the track through the forest passed over the brook flowing down from the copper mines into the marshland, which lies wet and slimy between the foot of the crags and the water of the lake. Hard by were the cots of the miners, and supereminent above them the house of the reeve set over them by the king. These folk the priest had in some measure induced to outward semblance of respect to holy days and the services of the church; but by long continuance amongst them and partaking of their uncivil ways, not being under obedience to canonical commands, he had as it were fallen asleep with none to awaken him.

And so when Cuthbert the holy man, hungered and weary with much travel, approached, he beheld this poor man sitting thus at the door of the cell that was his church, bearded unseemly and unbefittingly attired, while through rents in the walls things sacred were revealed to eyes profane, and the unthatched roof let in the droppings of birds who nested thereupon, to fall over the very altar. Which seeing, Cuthbert was moved to anger and compassion, saying "O dog of the Lord, why slumberest thou? Art thou then indeed one of those dumb dogs of whom it is written that they cannot bark? Arise and let thy voice be heard. Call thy flock together for the morrow that I may salve them."

And this being spoken in the tongue of the Irish which Cuthbert knew right well, roused the poor man, who blinked upon him and brought forth his bell, which was as it were an iron pot with a stone hanging therein by a rope of bark; and he began to rattle it. But none answered: for it was of a Saturday at evening, and all were in like manner ensnared with carnal feasting and sodden with ale.

Then the blessed Cuthbert sighed in spirit and went from house to house, seeking for himself and his men where to lay their heads. But none received him, for even the reeve said churlishly that he would have nought to do with strangers, be they who they might. So they came to the last cots in the village, and there was a very mean house, and a poor widow sitting at the door of it: who seeing the man of God rose up and made obeisance.

Now Cuthbert was tall of stature, of a long face and ruddy, but meagre with fasting: and yet of a countenance most benign, and shining as the sun; and his eyes were as bright as stars under thick brows that hung over them grey and bushy; and the bones of his brows were great and stood forward under the sloping field of his forehead. Upon his head he wore a lofty mitre glistening with crystal, and in his hand was the pastoral staff set with many pearls; and upon his robes were orphreys embroidered with thread of gold. Seeing this poor widow he blessed her and her house, and she bade him enter, for that such as she had was at his service.

Within the house, which was rudely framed of wattled boughs and thatched with broom, there was scant space for that company even to stand; and one of the disciples plucked the bishop by the sleeve, bidding him in a whisper beware of the foulness and contamination of so mean a dwelling. But Cuthbert smiled, and penetrating the darkness with his keen glance, beheld upon a bed of heather in the corner two children lying; the one a lad of tender years, and the other a babe. Their mother

34

prayed him to forgive their incapacity, for, said she "the lad has lamed himself in the mines where his father was killed a year ago, and the babe is sick, and there is no one can heal it."

Now of all men whose name has come to our understanding, this holy Cuthbert was most like to our Lord and Saviour in this, that he loved little children and was good to them: and none of his company wondered when he sat down, and taking the babe in his arms kissed it and blessed it: and it looked up to him and laughed, and in that hour the sickness was abated. And then he did in like manner to the lad, touching him and stroking his hurt, so that in a little while the pain went out of his limbs, and he stood up, and was utterly healed.

Then came running the daughter of the woman, with a vessel in her hand, and it was empty: for she had gone to find milk for the children, but no one would give to her: and so she returned weeping. But Cuthbert laid his hand on her head and blessed her, and bade her go to the well and draw water; and lo! when she poured, it was sweet as milk to the taste, and as new milk with the cream therein; so that this well was reckoned a holy well after that Cuthbert had done this miracle. And sitting down, some in the house and some at the door, the men drew from their wallets the crusts that remained, and they supped together, they and their hosts; and never was merrier supper nor better fare, when the holy man had blessed it.

Now when morning was come the noise of these doings

had gone forth, and a great company was awaiting the bishop, of these who over-night had despised and rejected him. First, he went to the little church, and there did the service in right order. Then, standing in the door, he spoke to the people with that eloquence and divine persuasiveness which many a time softened stony hearts in the recesses of Lodonian hills, and overawed the proud in the halls of Northumbrian lords and wealthy men and the satraps of the king.

And when he had done speaking they all with one consent lifted up their voices, these kneeling to him and those lifting up rough hands to heaven. As if moved by I know not what heavenly inspiration, some brought wood and timber, others axes and saws; yea, even the children plucked broom for roofing; and in an incredibly brief space of time, the reeve leading the way and labouring among them, having laid aside his cloak and trappings of dignity, the posts of a new and greater edifice were sunk in the earth, and the frame as it were of a fair church and house of assembly for all them of the village was marked out. For a while the priest stood by as one bewildered, and then in faltering words, "What do ye, my brethren?" he cried, "and ye Romans in this labour on the Lord's day, in which it is not lawful to do any manner of work?"

But the blessed Cuthbert looked smilingly upon him, saying "Rebuke them not; for the Sabbath was made for man, and not man for the Sabbath. This is a work of mercy, and of necessity. It is a gladness and no

36

labour, to build the Lord's house on the Lord's day."
And with that the priest himself, as if smitten with the
contagion of fervour, threw down his encumbering
garment at the bishop's feet, and fell to haling and
dragging of timber until the sweat dripped from his
temples.

So cheerfully they wrought that by sunset the new
house was roofed; and if not wholly finished nor a work
of perfect architecture, still serviceable and ready to be
consecrated : the which was done before the blessed
Cuthbert took his ways and went on his journey to the
region of Cartmel.

Now this is accounted the greatest miracle which St.
Cuthbert did in the land. For to heal the sick is a
great work, and to turn water into wine is a wonderful
thing; but no man by human wit and science alone
could impart to sordid souls the greatest of all spiritual
gifts, as then, when by divine grace, and the working of
heavenly might, he made churls charitable.

THE BOW IN THE CLOUD.

The floods were out at Coniston,
    And round the Waterhead
On road and meadow, hour by hour,
    The rising water spread.

It rained as it had never rained;
    It stormed,—at each alarm
The creaking fir-tree mopped and mowed,
    And waved a threatening arm.

And Yewdale crags were out of sight,
    It was so thick that day;
Only their falls like lightning-forks
    Glared white upon the grey.

Then Baby, from the window-sill,
    Peered out into the gloom,
With anxious eyes, as one who waits
    The very crack of doom.

" What is it then, my little one?
    Come down," the mother said;
" You'll scare yourself:"—for older folk
    Had cause to feel afraid.

" O mother, let me stay a while;
    The storm will soon be done,
I'll tell you when the rainbow comes, —
    You know there *will* be one."

*   *   *   *   *

Yes,—differences must be, while men
   Dwell on the outer form :
There must be strife, while flesh is weak
   And blood is quick and warm.

The only peace, the only truth
   Is that primeval faith
That holds the Promises of Good,
That looks for rainbow after flood
   And glory after death.

THE STORY OF THURSTAN AT THE THWAITE.

[The division of High Furness was made in the reign of Henry II., in the days of Abbot John Cantsfield. Dolfin of Kirkby and the rest, as well as the two monks, are historical characters,—all except the family at the Thwaite; which place nevertheless may have been a Norse settlement, probably the first Norse farmstead in our immediate neighbourhood.

It is true that no sagas were ever written here; but there must have been tales told by the Northmen's descendants which, had they been written down, would have fallen more or less into saga-form: thus:—]

CHAPTER I.

OF THE FOLK THAT DWELLED THERE.

Thurstan hight a man. He was Swainson: Swain was Thurstanson: and their fore-elder was Swain, the son of Thurstan of the Mere. He dwelt at the Thwaite; that is at Conyngs-tun in the land of Hougun, by the side of the mere that was his mere. He was a stout man and a strong man of his hands, but elderly, and stirred out little from his fields downbank along the waterhead and the garths on the how aback of his hall. For he saw the way things were going, and liked it not: being a man of the old sort, and not given to change. Most of all he hated King Stephen, though he had little love for King Henry that was: but ever a good word for the King of Scots, that had been reckoned overlord of these parts in his young days, and let folk be, with no talk of stirring old use and wont. Now the old use in these parts was that every man was his own man, and no king's man whosoever.

Thurstan wedded Gunnhild; she was Orm's daughter of Kirkeby nigh Gerlewarth; but she was dead. Their son was Swain, and their daughter was Ingiburg. Swain was a good farmer, but this grieved Thurstan, that his son should be ever after new fangled ways in farming.

CHAPTER II.

How the Kent-dale men came.

Now it was a day when men came to the Thwaite and asked guesting. None said nay, for many passed by that road, what with thingmen going to Little Langdale, what with cowper-lads and chapmen: there would be never a two-months' time but new faces came by, and all were welcome. So when they had bite and sup, says the head man of them, 'Well I know thee, master Thurstan, by name, and better would I know thee by nature.' With that says he, sitting easily in his high-seat, 'Little there is to know but what there is to see. I am an old man, in the old spot.' 'Well,' says the other, 'there is one I serve would be thy friend.' 'Good friends,' says he, 'are always good finding.' 'True,' says he, 'and this is a good friend and a bad foe.' 'I like him the better," says Thurstan at the Thwaite. 'They call him William of Lancaster,' the other went on. 'I like him the worse,' says Thurstan in his beard. '*Splendor Dex*,' says the stranger, 'but thou must like him or lump him.' 'And who art thou, thrall of him they call baron, to come knapping French at me?' Now this was Bernard the forester, and with him was his brother William, and they had a half-score of men with them. And they leaped up and rattled the arrows in their quivers. 'Peace, lads,' cried Thurstan, 'I bide no durdoms in my hall. Sit ye down, and sup mannerly. Are ye slockened? Then come with me and I will show ye somewhat.' With that he took his great hollin staff, and went forth of the door, going stiffly because of his age and of the sickness that was in his knee-joints : and led them up to his how aback of the hall, and bade them stand in the garth that was atop of the how, when you come out of the wood on the how-side. 'Look ye well," said he, waving the hollin wand around, so that they backed somewhat; 'Look ye well and see yon garths and fields, folds and cots, and the reek rising from the hall of the Thwaite. All this land,' said he thrusting the wand into the ground, "all this

land my fore-elders took when it was no-man's land.
All this land they cleared, and digged, and ploughed,
and tilled. All yon cots they built for their thralls : and
yon hall for themselves and their children. Two
hundred winters they have lived on this spot, and I
hold it now. Go back to your lord that calls himself a
Northman, and tell him this. If Northman he be, a
Northman's hand he shall have. If Frenchman he be,
my old knees are none so lish as they were.' And so
the men went back to Kent-dale very ill pleased ; but as
for the baron, men say he laughed at that word, and
was loath to take it ill.

CHAPTER III.

How two monks came to the Thwaite.

Now it was another day, and two monks came that
gate. They were clothed all in woollen, and wore white
kirtles that were long to the feet, and hoods and white
scarves they called scapulary, and over all, for the
weather was cold by now, black gowns to wrap them in.
Also they had boots, but gloves they wore none. And
the thralls gaped at them, but Thurstan gave them a
seat, and they broke bread, but flesh-meat they would
not so much as look at. Nevertheless they might drink
ale, and they drank it, but not much. So when they
were fed, they began to open out their business and it
seemed that the one was brother William of Leeds, he
who afterwards was cellerar in the Abbey of St. Mary's,

and the other was brother William of Lonsdale. 'Why,' says master Thurstan, 'it rains Williams nowadays. But no harm,' says he, 'since we like a sup of wet.' 'And get it,' says the monk. 'And thrive on it,' says Thurstan. 'For' says the monk, 'He sendeth it on the evil and the good.' 'So I have heard tell,' says Thurstan. 'Maybe ye think us heathens, but many's the time that word has been flung at my head by father John there, when we have had our little strifes:— easily settled, father John, easily settled, man, are they not?' 'It is well!' said the monk: 'for we of Holy Church love a man of worth that bows his neck to the yoke that is easy and light; and in that hope we come.' 'What now?' says Thurstan to the ale-horn, as it were. 'Our lord abbot and our house of St. Mary in Furness, by the grant of King Stephen of blessed memory'— 'Whom God forgive,' says the old one. 'It is well,' says the monk, 'for all men need it, and the prayer becomes all that can say it; but as I am bidden tell thee, our lord, knowing thee to be a true son of the Church,— though as yet lacking—we all lack, my good sir,— somewhat of perfection, our lord would have thee know that by such kingly grant this land is in his holding'— 'It was never a king's to give,' broke forth master Thurstan. 'Hear me, my good master, and hear a friend friendliwise. Our lord abbot is loath to use violence, as violent men of the world use. There be those yonder,' he went on, waving his hand to the morning-ward, 'would think no more of roof-burning and throat-cutting than of smoking a wolf out of his earth. Now of all such our men be free, for who dare touch the lands of Holy Church? Many, aye and thy own kin, they of Kirkeby, have come in to us: and what ask we of them? Burdens? Gifts? Shames? Nay, it is honour we show them, gifts we give them, their burdens, as the apostle bids, we bear. Ask master Dolfin thy brother, ask Orm, or any of the holders of the southlands: and be guided.' But for all answer looked master Thurstan across the hall and through the reek of the hearth, as one in a dream; and then slapping his right hand upon the arm of his seat, said he, 'See ye this old settle? Heart of oak it is, and black with eld. See ye yon rafters and balks? soot-blue they be, and even yet sound as a bell. See ye the smoke going up? For two hundreds of winters never has the spark died out on the hearth. Holy church we reverence; lords we love not: thralls we are not. And sooner than follow yon nithings to their shame, I would see the roof of my fathers in a low, and lie like a blue coal among the ashes.' So the monks went home and told the abbot, and he took it badly enough.

CHAPTER IV.

HOW THURSTAN'S HOUSE WAS DIVIDED.

So matters went on for that winter and no stir was made; for if the Abbot came in with force then he would have the baron against him, and if the baron sent his men against the folk of the fells, then the Abbot would complain of him to the King. But they went to work nevertheless, by words and promises and threats to bend the holders to their side and so get what they wanted; for it is said 'Possession is nine points of the law.' And in a while Swain Thurstanson says he is bidden to Kent-dale to guest with the baron there; and with much grumbling from his father, off he goes in his best clothes; and back he came, boasting of the friendliness of my lord, and the kindness of my lady, and the new ways of hunting and the weapons he had seen: until his old father bade him hold his peace for a fool. And then must Ingiburg away to the abbey for what father John called a pilgrimage for the good of her soul; and will he, nill he, Thurstan must give her horse and horseman to ride withal; and back she came chattering like a jay of the fair great houses of the monks, and their chapel so rich with carven work and gold and gems, and the singing of the choir, and the preaching of one that spoke to the heart, and the goodness of all the holy men, and their sufferings at the hands of worldly folk—'Like me,' growls Thurstan at the Thwaite. And so he abode like one betwixt two fires, or a balk of timber men are bringing to a house-building, when the oxen are unruly and pull two ways at once.

CHAPTER V.

DOINGS AT THE THING.

Now midsummer was come, and men rode to the Thing as of old use and wont. For matters of the countryside were still talked over at the old spot in Little Langdale, and folk met there year by year for their sports and their speaking, however it were of little avail. And this time it was said there would be talk of this new business, namely the business of the abbot and the baron and their striving for the fell country. So thither rides Thurstan at the Thwaite with his men; and there he finds his kinsmen Dolfin and Ulf of Kirkeby, and Orm of Ourgrave, and Ailward of Broughton, and Gillemichael of Merton and Orm Bernulfson of Urswick, and Siward and Ketel and others of the old stock, such as had gone under the abbot, because they lived near at hand to him, and feared the Church, and saw what was coming. But with these old Thurstan would have nought to do, and when they spoke friendly he passed them by. And when the business was opened, they spoke for the Abbot and praised his rule, and their lot, and threatened all gainsayers with the ban of the Church, and house-burning and man-slaying. Then spoke up the men out of Westmorland, from Ambleside way and Bronulf's head and Kent-dale and the Lyth, and they were for the baron, bidding the fell-folk think on his might and wealth; for, said they, he could crush the whole tale of

47

them as a lad cracks a nut in his teeth. And then the old man held up his hand to speak. He was tottering with eld and with wrath : and the words clove to his tongue; and he stood there white and angry, being a laughing-stock to all. But before speech could come of him, there was thrusting among the crowd, and into it pressed a little man, in a long gown, swordless and beardless : but behind him was a company of billmen and bowmen, no folk of the fells, and around and about the Thingstead rode a many men on great horses, mailed and helmed, with long spears, and painted shields, and one of them bare a banner, and it was the banner of King Henry. And the little man, going boldly up, stood on the mount, and cried out shrilly as one who speaks a strange tongue, and mockingly as one who has his foe at his foot : and he said 'By your leave, good men and liege men all; by the leave of this good company whatsoever it calls itself: the king speaks: hear the word of the king.' And so he fell to reading off a scroll in Latin, and setting it out in English bit by bit, as a lad does with his grammar-task :—
'*Henricus*, Henry, *Dei gratia*, by the grace of God, *rex Angliæ*, King of England, and so forth and so forth. *Sciatis omnes*, know ye all, *ad quos*, to whom, *præsentes litteræ*, these present letters, *pervenerint*, may come, and so forth. *Inspeximus cartam*, we have seen the charter—friends, by your leave I pretermit the Latin, which is here for your learned inspection, and come to the business in plain terms. The king sayeth, he confirms

the grant of Stephen Earl of Boulogne and Mortaigne and late king of England, to the abbot and monks of St. Mary in Furness, giving them all his forest of Furness and Wagheney, and so forth and so forth. Likewise our lord the king hath seen and does hereby confirm the grant from the honour of Westmorland to William of Lancaster of the barony of Kent-dale, and so forth. And whereas a certain land or lands, being forest and debateable ground is or are in dispute betwixt the two, namely the abbey of Furness and the barony of Kent-dale, and whereas for the better holding of the king's peace and the settlement of this realm it is reasonable and proper that such dispute should be determined :—Now therefore the king commands and ordains that thirty good men and true, being well acquainted with such land or lands, namely, the lands in dispute between the Abbey of St. Mary's in Furness and the Barony of Kent-dale, do appear before commissioners as hereby constituted and hereinafter appointed, and there and then make oath that they will truly and justly and equally survey apportion and divide the land or lands in the dispute herebefore mentioned : and that such division being made and determined the parties thereto are hereby summoned—' 'What says the chattering con, in a tongue a man may hear?' quoth Thurstan to his son. 'Thus much I gather, that they have netted the boar and will forthwith flay him.' And when folk saw a young man leading an old one, they made way, seeing that he was sick to death.

Chapter VI.

Of the withstanding in Yewdale beck.

Thurstan at the Thwaite sat on his how that is aback
of his hall, in the garth that is on the how, as you come
out of the woods on the how side. Thurstan sat there on
a rigg of stone that comes up out of the turf, and the
stone is blue stone, but is waved in the bait like sand
of the sea strand: and that stone is there to this day.
Thurstan had let do on him his sword, that was his
father's and his father's father's sword before him: and
he loosened the strings from the sheath and laid it
athwart his knees. And no man spoke to him. In
Yewdale all was still. But about noontide when the
sun was bright there was a flickering in the trees of
Yewdale, where Yewdale beck comes out from betwixt
Raven crag and Yewdale crag: and in a while a
company of people was seen, some a-foot, some a-horse,
coming down the beck bottom as it were down a road.
Now these were the company of the thirty men, who
had taken oath to divide the land of the fells according
to the bidding of Henry: and their dividing was on
this wise. First they compassed the country round
about, beginning even from Little Langdale, and going
by the Broadwater, that is Brathay, to the head of
Winandermere, and thence by Leven to Greenodd.
And then they made the boundary from the Thingstead
to Wreneshause and so down the Duddon to Broughton
and the sands. And lastly they halved the land so

50

marked out; for they came beating the bounds from the Brathay to Tillesburgthwaite, and from Tillesburgthwaite down Yewdale beck and so to the head of Thurstan's water, and down the farther shore of Thurstan's water to Crake. But by now they were come into Yewdale: and the array of their company was seen flashing and moving in the noonday sunlight in the dale betwixt the crags and the woods wherein the Tarns are. Which when the old man saw, he stood up, and held his sword in his right hand, and passing out of the garth-door he went slowly down the hill that was his howe, and stood in the beck that was his beck, wading knee-deep in the brown water, and standing there so still that the trout nestled and nosed against his knees. When suddenly by a bend of the river the foremost of the thirty sworn men came in sight, and it was Dolfin of Kirkeby, who knowing that land right well was the guide and leader in their wayfaring. And he was the brother of Thurstan's wife. Whom when Thurstan saw he bade him stand and asked him by what right he thus entered his land with men not unarmed. 'Brother', said he,—'No brother,' cried the old man, 'I know thee not, if thou be not that nithing of the Northmen, that thrall of the monks, that betrayer of thy kin—' 'Peace, old man,' cried they all, 'and let the king's warrant pass.' 'Fiend take ye all,' shrieked the old man, and his eyes were flashing and his face trembling. 'Foul fall your king, and you, ye dastards, nithings all'; and he spat upon them, and heaved up his brand to fall upon the fore-

most, crying out with a great cry.   But even in that cry
he fell, and lay there flat in the water : and when men
stooped to lift him up there was no life in him.

CHAPTER VII.

OF THE BURYING OF THURSTAN.

After that went Swain Thurstanson to Dalton to
speak with the priest there of the burying of his father
that was dead.   For folk of these parts must go even so
far to get kirk-burial.   But the priest, he was brother to
the Abbot of Furness, said that one who had fallen in
resisting the church and the king's men, and with ill
words in his mouth, should have no Christian burial at
his hands.   And so they buried him on his how, and
poor folk wept for him.   And so ends the story.

THE BALLAD OF YOUNG BEAUMONT.

[In the time of Edward III., Sir John Elland, sheriff in Yorkshire,
attacked Quarmby Hall and slew Sir Robert Beaumont. His two
boys and widow went to Towneley in Lancashire and Brereton in
Cheshire, where they lived until the lads were grown up. Then,
with young William Lockwood, son of another victim of Elland,
they met Lacy, Dawson, and Haigh at Cromwellbottom near Brig-
house, and killed Elland; after which they fled to Furness Fells
(1346). In or about 1363 they returned to Yorkshire, and tried to
recover their patrimony, but were set upon by the people and slain
(Whitaker's, "Loidis and Elmete," III. 396). In 1346 the Fleming
of Coniston was Sir John, who was succeeded in 1353 by his elder
son Richard.

The ballad is such as would give the tradition of our local Robin
Hood, after some generations had blurred and confused it. In
1350-60 there was probably no park, though there were deer: there
were no tall chimneys, though there was a Coniston Hall: and it is
not certain what was the age of the Springs bloomery, though I
think it may have been in working about the time of the story].

When grass was green and shaws were sheen
   Young Adam o' Beaumont's gone
To hunt the roe and the fallow doe
   In the park of Cunningston.

For he has slain the proud Elland
   That did his father quell,
And he has fled with his merry-men all
   To the woods of Furness Fell.

There's Adam, and his young brother,
  And Lacy, and Lockwood's Will,
And Dawson tough, and Haigh o' the Clough
  That the sheriff's life did spill.

And they have ta'en to the Furness Fells
  Their outlawry to bide,
But little they reck of the outlaw's doom
  And little their deeds they hide.

In Satterthwaite they housed them
  In a safe and sure bigging,
All for to drive the Abbot's deer
  And the deer of the proud Fleming.

So now when dew was white on grass
  Or ever the morn was red,
They tripped so light o'er Grizedale moor
  And turned the Waterhead,
And the granger woke as he heard them pass
  And cuddled him closer in bed.

Fowl and folk were sound asleep,
  Toft and town were dark,
And Coniston hall was steeked and still
  When they brake into Coniston park.

Swiftly ran the good greyhound,
  And sharply twanged the bow,
And for every flight the arrow flew
  A hart was lying alow.

"Come, big we here a bright bonfire,
　And brittle a hart o' greece :
Hold now your hand, my brethren dear,
　And break your fast in peace.

"Here's venison steaks would feast a duke
　And drink that never will fail,—
It is my proper tap," quoth he,
　"For they call it Adam's ale !"

　　　*　　　*　　　*　　　*

Sir John he waked and Sir John he winked ;
　"Is the laithe afire "? quoth he,
"Nay, nay, Sir John, 'tis a pitstead reeks ;
　Lig whyat," said his lady.

Dickon looked out, the young Fleming,
　And Robin looked out, his fere ;
And as they stood at the grey garth-yett
　A laugh on the breeze they hear.
"The woodland thieves are breaking our park,
　And taking our fallow deer !"

Forth they went with their meinie,
　They were six men and a score ;
"Now will ye fight or will ye flee?
　For we be twenty more !"

Adam he drew a good yew bow,
　And Will, and his fellows all ;
But a score still stood in a laund of the wood
　Though six of the foe should fall.

"A boat, a boat," cried young Lacy,
    And "A boat," cried wily Will :
"Now stand, ye rogues," cried Robin and Dick,
    "We'll be upsides with ye still !"

By Thurston water there's a spot—
    Ye'll ken the Springs for sure ;—
Where smithy folk should land a boat
    For leading of the ure.

"Cut her adrift, lads !" Adam he cried,
    "I'll hold them while ye board."
But even as she took the waterway
    He's fallen on the lairy sward.

"A rescue, a rescue !" cried they then,
    And backed upon the oar ;
But up there came the Fleming's men
    And he's down beneath a score.

"Now fare ye well, my merrymen all,
    Farewell till the morrow's morn !"
"We'll stop thy false tongue," Dickon he growled,
    And gagged his mouth in scorn.

* * * *

Sir John sat on his high ha' seat :
    "Now fetch the rascal here,
To be judged for shooting of my men
    And for slaughtering of my deer.

" For these two deeds that thou hast done
    It is each a felony :
So think to-night upon thy sins,
    And to-morn on the hangman's tree."

The gag was rugging at his teeth,
    His hands and feet were fast,
And beards wagged all in Coniston hall
    For they'd ta'en the thief at last.

And never a soul would rue the morn
    But one, her name I'll tell,
That was the lady's bower-maiden
    And they called her Kirsty Bell.

It was Kirsty here and Kirsty there,
    And " Kirsty, fill for me ; "
But aye as he sat on the rushen floor
    He followed her with an e'e.

So light of foot, so fair of face,
    And a look so soft and kind ;
" And O," thinks he, "could I win me forth
    She never should bide behind."

Sir John was merry, the lady laughed,
    And Dickon and Rob 'gan sing :
" Lass, take yon knave a sup of ale
    For a health to our lord the king :
It will put him in heart to play his part
    O' the morn," says the proud Fleming.

" How can he speak, if his mouth be stopped?"
   Says Dick, "Take out the gag."
" How can he stand if his feet be fast?"
   Says Rob, "Then let them wag."

" How can he drink if his hands be tied?"
   "Why so!" says Kirsty Bell,
And sned the cord with a carving-knife
   Or ever the shouting fell.

The bicker was in his left hand,
   And the whittle was in his right:
" Here's to the king!" cried Adam Beaumont,
   " And the lads I'll meet to-night!"

O, and folk were fain to flee
   When they saw yon whittle shine,
But their feet were ali in a snarl with ale
   And their eyes were mazed with wine.

And man! there was a durdom
   Or ever they cleared the hall:
There were folk aneath the table board
   And up the chimney tall.

" Away, away, my bonny lad,
   It is no time to laik!"
" But will ye 'gree, and flit with me?
   Or never a step I take!"

He's clipt her up betwixt his arms
  As a shepherd carries a lamb,
And they're afloat in the little cock-boat
  The bainest gate for heam.

And whiles she'd laugh, and whiles she'd greet,
  And the stars shone bright aboon;
And eh! but life and love were sweet
  By the light of a hunter's moon.

THE HERMIT OF MONK CONISTON.

[It is often asked by readers of the late Dr. Gibson's "Ramblings and Ravings round the Old Man," whether his "legends" are founded on fact, or mere inventions of his own. That of the hermit at Bank ground was based on a tradition preserved by the old statesman-family there, who used to show a well which, like another between Far End and the village, had some repute as a holy well. It is likely that there was a hermit, or more than one in succession, on the spot where the Bankes family afterwards made their "Ground." As a set-off to the rollicking nineteenth-century tale of "Father Brian," I have tried to sketch the portrait of a real hermit, from authentic records.

In the middle of the fourteenth century certain Yorkshire nuns wrote the life of Richard Rolle, of Hampole, preacher, author and hermit. They prepared it in the form of an "office" or service to be used in celebrating his feast-day, for they hoped that the Pope would canonize him, as indeed was well deserved; for no man has ever written more nobly of the love of God and the life of the Christian than Richard Rolle; he was one of those born saints who were a real blessing to their age. Whether the nun's petition never reached the Pope, or whether the Devil's Advocate prevailed, we know not. Richard is not on the Calendar; but his Life and Works remain, in mediæval English and mediæval Latin, to show us what a real hermit might be, if we need assurance that the faith was not without witnesses in an age we call dark and erring.

Fancy, then, for a moment, that another such lived here; and that the house of Furness put in their claim for him. On this wise, in the florid Latin of their day, they would have written].

FRAGMENT FROM AN UNEDITED MS. OF FURNESS ABBEY.

That blessed John, who for the honied sweetness of his eloquence and the golden sentences of his wisdom may rightly be called a second Johannes Chrysostomus, was born in a certain city of the meridional parts of *England*; but his parents being of the north country and loving the mountainous rudeness of this their fatherland more than the urbane enjoyments of the south, brought him yet a child into these regions. By the which habitude and early dwelling beside the out-spread waters of our lakes and beneath the wooded rocks of remoter valleys, there was instilled into him such awe of the divine wonders of the desert wilds, which to many another are but a terror and a stumbling-block, that even in his infantile age he sang with rare sweetness the glories of the Creator in these his manifold and marvellous works.

Ps. *Levavi oculos* etc.*

Nor was his mind on other matters uninformed; for by the industry of his parents he was set to learn the rudiments of worldly letters: and being proficient in Latin was put to the university of *Oxford*, where he studied, not without praise and early reputation. There-after voyaging in foreign parts from town to town of *Gallia* and *Burgundia* even unto the holy city, he sought the converse of the learned and the study of such things as remain from ancient times, in order to perfect himself in arts and sciences both humane and divine. And in due course being made Doctor and Teacher in the said University, by his eloquence he

---

*These psalms and hymns are intended to be sung to enliven and vary the collation or reading of the office upon the feast-day of the saint.

attracted, by his exhortations improved, and by his erudition informed the studious youth who flocked to him, together with many of their elders, both in *Oxford* and elsewhere, in whatsoever place he appeared, another Abelardus, teaching and preaching a spiritual philosophy.* Admirable indeed and profitable were this wonderful man's outpourings and sacred illustrations, with which he brought many a hearer out of darkness into light; and moreover in his mellifluous tractates and books composed for the edification of the world, how many a period still re-echoes the sweetest harmony in the souls of those that have read with understanding; how many a word of warning still rolls its thunders in the quaking hearts of those that have heard, and trembled at the storm of his righteous indignation.

[Here follow verses in praise of his eloquence].

Now when many years had been consumed in these labours, and his bodily strength was somewhat abated, though not the fire of a spirit ever ardent after the secrets of divine life and the mysteries of the divine working, this blessed man, having regard to the saying of the apostle "Lest when I have preached," etc., bethought himself of retirement from the world. And quitting the scene of his triumphs, and disparting his goods among the poor, he denuded himself of gold and silver, giving to these precious stones, and to those his books and images of price; thus laying up greater and

*The passage following is closely copied from the Life of Richard, showing that it was known to the Furness scribe.

more enduring treasure in heaven. Of all rules of religion he chiefly esteemed the Cistercian, not for learning, nor for power, but being led by his philosophy, not falsely so called, toward the virtue of bodily toil and the felicities of pastoral life in which the Cistercians do exercise themselves, fulfilling the command " In the sweat of thy brow," etc. For in this rule he found rightly balanced and intermixed the Contemplative with the Active, and the double blessing of faith and works enjoyed. So being come with the remnant of that he had to *Furness*, he was received with joy, as one about to do honour to the place of his adoption with his substance and his fame, and to edify men with the example of his life and the wisdom of his teaching.

[Verses in praise of the Cistercian rule].

Thus remaining for a space in all humility and yet in labour abundant, it seemed that he might be chosen to high place,—yea, even to end his days in the dignities of Lordship and the chair of the Abbot. But for our faults this was not permitted; and for his own greater glory hereafter greater things were in store for him. There is a certain piece of water within the liberties of the lordship of St. Mary's, by name the water of Turstinus, or in the English tongue *le Thorstane's watter*. Around this lake stand huge and well nigh inaccessible mountains, and especially along the oriental shores of it arise steep hills thickly beset with ancient trees, such as oaks, beeches, hollies, and so forth. None inhabit there, saving it be wood-cutters and hearth-men in the service of our Lord Abbot, for the burning of iron ore which they carry thither on the backs of horses from pits in *Alinschales* and *Ourgrave* and elsewhere. But on the adverse coast lie certain houses of the tenants of St. Mary's at a place called *le Thwait*, and beyond the water of *Ywedallbec* is *Conyngeston* and the hall of a good knight, father at the time of Sir John Fleming, who now holds of our Lord.* Else all is desert and forest land, until you come to *Haukensheved* at the farther side of certain mountains. Now with permission of our lord, and conducted by men who knew the land, is the blessed Johan come to the water and brought in a boat to the farthest headland of the shore, and there set down, with little pomp, in the thickest part of the wood, beyond that region which the colliers and workers of iron had heretofore penetrated. It was surely by some providence that he found even in these wilds a little hut, left by a certain wood-cutter, and empty, though ruinous and hardly keeping the rain from his body. The which by labour being restored into some fitness of use, he inhabited, requiring little and content with that which others scorned.

[More verses, so barbarous as to be untranslatable].

Many are the wonderful histories yet in the mouths of all, concerning the deeds of this blessed man; how he dwelt there alone, improving the solitude with heavenly converse and wrestling with the demons which infest

---

*This fixes the date; for there were two Sir Johns, father and son, of whom the second died 1353.

the darkness of the waste. For victual he had that which the wood afforded him, and the little plot of land which with his own hands, the rough growth of wildings being eradicated, he tilled and set with fruit and herbs. Moreover they of the place, knowing that a sanctity had come upon their homes through his presence, would visit him with their little offerings of a fish, or a handful of meal; and from the hither bank of the water would come in their boats the children of the neighbours dwelling at *le Thwait* and round about: whom he received gladly, telling them indeed but little of that philosophy for which he had been sought, and was still famed, but things suited to their infantile understanding, as one who had learned the secrets of the world and set no store by them. For he taught them of herbs and healing things, such as he had in daily habitude before his eyes, as the Scripture says, "From the cedar tree," etc. And beasts, and fowl, and creeping things were his brethren, resorting to him; and as Adam in the Paradise, he welcomed them each by name, knowing well their ways and needs. Yea, even the elements were obedient to him. For there is a certain spring of water . . . .

[The rest of the story is hardly decipherable. It seems to refer to the miracle by which the virtues of this holy-well were established, and goes on to relate the hermit's dealings with the Fleming family: how the elder son William was struck with an incurable disease, and the daughter Joan was married to John le Towers of Lowick, which we know happened in 1333. There is mention of two tenants of the Lowick family, Thomas Scale and Nicholas Child, and — *cætera desunt*].

THE LEAGUER OF CARLISLE.

[It is told in the book of the Reverend Hugh Todd, Doctor in
Divinity, and sometime a prebendary of Carlisle, how the Scots, in
the year 1382, having burnt Penrith and a part of Carlisle, were put
to flight by the appearance of a great army, which was shown them
by a lady, thought to be "ye blessed Virgin Mary ye patroness of
ye citty": for which cause "her impress wth our Saviour in her
arms is ye publick seale of ye corporacon to this day."]

"O yonder comes a wetherlamb,
    And yonder comes a yowe,
And yonder comes a young lad,—
    And what's the tidings now?
Young man, shepherd lad,
    Whistling blithe and gay,
Wi' the white ling in thy bonnet,
    It is good news to-day?"

"O lasses, harken hither,
    It's tidings, and it's true,—
Doings of a lady fair
    That never man could do."
"Nay then, shepherd lad,
    Sit thee down and tell;
A tale's a tale i' Dunnerdale,
    So far beyond the fell."

" Ye kent the Scots were raiding ? "—
    " Nay, how should we be told ? "—
" And Perith Castle was a-lowe ? "—
    " Good Lord, they waxen bold."—
" And when they co' till Carlisle town
    They kessen fire therein.
They burnt a street "—" Eh, lady sweet !
    They wrought a deadly sin ! "

" Now fair befall your faces,
    And fair's the word ye say ;
And fair is yonder lady
    That keeps the town to-day."—
" Young lad, shepherd lad,
    Thy riddle's hard at read ! "—
" It's she that stands for merry Carlisle
    And who so good at need ?

" It was about the gloaming,
    And folk were all foredone
With hungering sore and fighting hard
    From dawn till set o' sun ;
The leaguer of the Scottish thieves
    Was round about the town,
And to-night, said they, or break of day
    Yon towers shall topple down.

" And it was about the gloaming
    A lady mought they spy,
A barn she bare on her arm so fair
    And softly tripped she by.

67

Stand! they cried, and Yield thee now!
　But she ever smiled the more :—
Good men, I seek wi' your chief to speak
　For need is passing sore.—

" Thy errand!—Will ye know it,
　My errand? answered she.
Then turn you round and gaze a stound
　Yonder on Haribee !—
And lo ! upon the landward edge
　They saw a ferly thing,
A grand array, as clear as day,
　And the banner of the king !

" No more they stayed for babe nor maid
　When that ferly thing they spied,
But Devil tak' the hindermost !
　Was all the bravest cried.
And this ran and that ran,
　Though heart and heartstrings crack ;
Till Esk was won and flight was done
　They never looked aback.

" It was the castle warder
　And he looked from Carlisle wall,
The red was on the little clouds
　And the night began to fall.
He saw the host on Haribee,
　He saw the lady speak,
He saw the Scot flit o'er the wath
　Like sparkles through the reek.

" He blew a note on his bugle-horn,
    And up the newel-stair
Who skips amain but Sir Captain?
    Who puffs but Master Mayor?
And bells ring out, and windows shine,
    And the bishop in golden weed,
He cries to the folk in the Minster aisle,—
Our Lady stands for Merry Carlisle,
    And who so good at need?"

        *   *   *   *

Now gloze the marvel as you may,
    Or deem it all a lie,
But so the town was kept and saved
    Five hundred years gone by.
And hardy heads of Cumbrian breed,
    And hands that loved a sword,
For Carlisle's public seal decreed
To grave, in memory of the deed,
These, whom they knew their best at need,
    Their Lady, and their Lord.

69

EPILOGUE.

Dosta mind when we were barns, brother, what holiday
laiks we had,
When thoo was nobut a lile un, and I was a mandrin'
lad,
And they sent us away fra Lirple, set lowse from tewin'
at school,
For lonterin' months o' summer and rattlin' weeks o'
Yule?
Eh, t' brecks we had togither, and t' ald spots ivery yan
By t' side o' Winthermer watter,—dosta mind them,
Davie man?

For now thoo's nea mair t' lile un.   They tell ma thoo's
coomt on fine,—
What, coach and six horses is nowt tull't, ner t' lectric
raalay line !
And folk co's bock o'er t' ocean and cracks o' thy dewin
wi' praise,
Sea happen thou's gitten o'er grand-like at care for t'
ancient days.
Bit naya, lad! I'se uphod it, thoo's nin sic a nowt-at-dowe
As forgits ald days, ald friends,—though it's thretty
year sen by now.

What ! wer rambles i' coppy and larch-wood, wer clims
i' t' cherry-tree,
Wer trots i' t' bock-loan sna when a blaazan moon
was hee ;

Eftherneans i' t' laithe or t' boathus-loft, wi' chips and
hammer and nails,
Conthriving a deck for t' centreboord, or cutting a suit
o' sails ;
And neets by a girt chat fire, wi' daame cooking
poddish and tates,
And ald Billy a-spinnin' his yarns while he fettled his
trolling-baits.

Sic teals as he used at tell us,—and a many he kent,
dud Will ;
There was Hugh, t' giant o' Troutbeck, and Adam o'
Rattlegill,
Rows wi' Scotch Rebels, he co'd 'em, and Forness
monks lang sen,
And t' Bassick boggle, and t' Beech-hill yan,—there
was boggles i' plenty then.
He's gone now, poor ald Billy, and t'dame, and t' good
ald folk ;
And many's t' change sen I and ye sat under his
rannal-boak.

Why, I's gitten ald mysel, and it's my turn now for a
yarn ;
And we've beath on us barns o' wer own, and nowt
caps teals for a barn.
If it's nobut an ald hair-reap, will ye tak it wi' love fra
heam ?—

For it's twined on t' seam ald creaks, and a deal o' t'
    stuff's t' seam :
If it's telt in a heamly way, as t' ald folk used at crack,
Then read it as thoo knas how : thoo's scan finnd
    trick co' back.

Happen it's fond, but I'm fain at a reet warm spot sud
    bide
I' t' brust o' thy barns for a heam on t' round world
    riper side.
It's grand, where t' Southern Cross leets up their sky of
    a lowe,
Yet t' Wain rolls round wer northern fells in a land o'
    long ago :
It's bonny, their garden-bower of a summery Kirsmas-
    day,
But ye were young where t' sweet-gale grows, sea far
    and far away.

www.ingramcontent.com/pod-product-compliance
Lightning Source LLC
Chambersburg PA
CBHW030000030726
47499CB00008B/2833